Ursel Scheffler

The Man with the Black Glove

illustrated by Christa Unzner

translated by Rosemary Lanning

North-South Books / New York / London

Copyright © 1999 by Nord-Süd Verlag AG, Gossau Zürich, Switzerland
First published in Switzerland under the title *Der Mann mit dem schwarzen Handschuh*
English translation copyright © 1999 by North-South Books Inc.

First published in the United States, Great Britain, Canada,
Australia, and New Zealand in 1999 by North-South Books,
an imprint of Nord-Süd Verlag AG, Gossau Zürich, Switzerland.
First paperback edition published in 2001.

Distributed in the United States by North-South Books Inc., New York.

Library of Congress Cataloging-in-Publication Data is available.
A CIP catalogue record for this book is available from The British Library.

ISBN 0-7358-1178-4 (TRADE BINDING)
1 3 5 7 9 TB 10 8 6 4 2
ISBN 0-7358-1179-2 (LIBRARY BINDING)
1 3 5 7 9 LB 10 8 6 4 2
ISBN 0-7358-1417-1 (PAPERBACK)
1 3 5 7 9 PB 10 8 6 4 2
Printed in Belgium

For more information about our books,
and the authors and artists who create them,
visit our web site: www.northsouth.com

A NORTH-SOUTH PAPERBACK

Critical praise for

The Man with the Black Glove

"Young detective Martin Pitman, first seen in Scheffler's *The Spy in the Attic*, has two new mysteries to solve in this easy chapter book. . . . The story moves quickly and the plot threads come neatly together at the climax."

School Library Journal

"Humorous dialogue and amusing . . . illustrations set a light tone for this fast-paced mystery. With abundant sketches throughout, this inviting chapter book will satisfy budding sleuths and readers of the first book in the series."   *Booklist*

Contents

1 A New Case?

Martin tugged Pauline's sleeve. "Hey! Look at him!" he whispered.

A man with a silver briefcase was running along the path outside her grandmother's house. The man glanced around to see if anyone was following him, then ducked through the hedge.

He didn't see the two children perched above him in the cherry tree.

"Did you see that?" asked Martin excitedly. "Very suspicious, don't you think?"

Pauline shrugged. "A man in a hurry," she said. "So what?" She picked some more cherries and stuffed them in her mouth.

The man reappeared further along the path. He dashed into a shed.

"Look! He broke into that shed," said Martin.

"No, he didn't. He had a key," said Pauline calmly.

"But why would he take a silver briefcase into a shed?" said Martin stubbornly. "This calls for a bit of detective work."

Pauline took a deep breath. "If you want to play detective, Martin Pitman," she said, "you can count me out. Don't you remember how stupid we looked last time, when we told everyone that Mr. Leon was a spy?"

"OK, OK," said Martin. "But I have a hunch about this. There's definitely something fishy going on."

"And I have a hunch I'll be in trouble if I'm not home soon," said Pauline. "It's almost lunchtime." She started to climb down.

"Stop! Don't move," hissed Martin.

The man was coming out of the shed— without the briefcase!

The man ran under their tree and disappeared through the hedge. He jumped into a blue van and started the engine. Martin slid down the tree, ran over to the hedge, and peered through.

He could just make out the plate number on the van as it roared away. He rummaged in his pocket, found a pencil stub and an old movie ticket, and wrote down the number. The van's wheels had left tracks on the dusty road, and beside them lay a black glove. Martin picked it up.

2 Lost Property

Martin put the glove in his pocket. "This could be evidence!" he muttered.

"Evidence of what?" asked Pauline. "The man didn't steal anything. He brought something with him, and left it here."

"You never can tell," said Martin. "When something's not quite right, a detective feels it in his bones."

"Come on," said Pauline impatiently. "We've got to get a move on."

They were running uphill, beside the canal.

"Not so fast!" wheezed Martin.

He stopped, and bent over to ease a stitch in his side.

"Hey, look what I found!" he shouted, and ran after Pauline, waving a brown leather wallet.

Pauline looked annoyed as she waited for Martin to catch up. "Having a friend who's a detective is nothing but trouble," she grumbled.

"But look! It's someone's wallet!" said Martin. He wiped the dirt off his find and showed it to her.

"Is there anything in it?"

"Wow!" said Martin. "Look at all this money!"

"We're rich!" said Pauline. "I take back what I said about detectives."

"We can't just keep it, can we?" said Martin.

"Well . . ." Pauline looked unsure.

Martin put the wallet away. "I'll ask my mother," he said.

He asked her as soon as he got home.

"You must hand it over to the police," she said firmly.

Martin was disappointed.

"I expect you'll get a reward," said his mother. "Besides, this wallet looks so old and tatty, it must belong to someone who badly needs the money."

"Hmm, who is supposed to be the detective around here?" said Martin, writing a big, red, raspberry-jam question mark in a bowl of custard.

As soon as he had finished his meal, Martin ran downstairs to Pauline's. "We have go to the police!" he yelled.

"Why do you want the police?" asked Mrs. Conner, shocked.

"I found a wallet," Martin told her. "With lots of money in it. My mother says we've got to hand it in."

"OK. Let's go," said Pauline.

3   At the Police Station

"Hello, I'm Sergeant Paterson. How can I help you?" said the man at the police station. He looked surprised when Martin thrust a wallet under his nose.

"I found it by the canal," said Martin. "At twelve twenty-four this afternoon."

"There's a lot of money in it," said Pauline.

"Well, bless me!" said the sergeant. "I wish all children were as honest as you two."

Martin and Pauline felt rather proud. It was a nice feeling. Almost as good as getting a reward.

"How do we find out who it belongs to?" asked Pauline.

Sergeant Paterson examined the lost property closely.

"I'm afraid there's nothing here to tell us who the owner is," he said after a while.

"How about this?" asked Martin. "Look . . . it's a ticket from the Blue Angel. That's a dry cleaner. My mother always goes there."

"Yes, but there's no name on it," the sergeant muttered. "Just a number—6063."

"But if the dry cleaner pulls out the clothes with that number, maybe she'll remember who brought them in," said Martin.

"Good thinking!" said the sergeant.

"All the other receipts are from Mega Mart," said Pauline thoughtfully. "Why don't we put a photo of the wallet at the supermarket door, and ask if anyone has lost it?"

"That might cause a riot, children. Hundreds of people would turn up and claim it," said the sergeant.

"We could say that only people who know what clothes they took to the cleaners last week should apply," suggested Martin.

"Good idea," said Sergeant Paterson. "I see we have a budding detective here."

"What if no one claims it?" asked
Martin.

"After a year, the money would be
yours."

Martin thought about this for a few
seconds. Then he said, "We'll try and
trace the owner anyway."

"Good luck!" said the sergeant, giving
them a thumbs-up.

4 Inquiries at the Blue Angel

The dry cleaner called the Blue Angel was owned by Mrs. Angela Marks.

Martin put the receipt on the counter.

"But your mother picked up her cleaning yesterday!" Mrs. Marks exclaimed.

"This thing doesn't belong to us. It's someone else's," Martin said.

"In that case I shouldn't really give it to you . . ."

"We could get a note from Sergeant Paterson to say it's all right," said Pauline quickly. "We're making inquiries, you see."

"We just want to know what it is, really," said Martin.

"All right. I'll have a look."

Mrs. Marks took the ticket.

She tapped the number 6063 into her computer. "That's the one," she said. Then she took a pole and lifted an old-fashioned brown coat off the conveyor belt on the ceiling.

"Do you remember who brought this coat in?" asked Martin.

"It must have been last Saturday . . . ," said Mrs. Marks, thinking aloud.

Martin examined the coat with his magnifying glass.

"What's the problem?" snapped Mrs. Marks. "We always do a thorough job!"

Even so, Martin found a hair in a fold of the sleeve.

It was a dog hair. No doubt about it.

"Do you remember someone with a black-and-white dog?" he asked.

"Mmm, yes, I do," said Mrs. Marks. "There was an old lady with a dog. She had some kind of a stick or a cane, I can't remember exactly, but whatever it was I do remember she dropped it. And the dog was outside, barking. Sorry. That's all I know. Now I must get to work."

"We should get ourselves ID cards from Sergeant Paterson," said Martin. "So people will know we're official detectives and take us seriously."

"And we need an assistant or two," Pauline said.

"Do you mean Philip and Julia?"

"Of course! You always tell me eight eyes see more than four!"

5 Official Detectives

"Well done," said Sergeant Paterson
the following day, when they reported on
their inquiries at the Blue Angel.
He was willing to give them an ID card.
On it he wrote:

*I hereby grant permission to
Mr. Martin Pitman to make
inquiries on my behalf, in the
case of "The Lost Property."*

The sergeant signed the card and
stamped it.

"Could I . . . ," said Pauline hesitantly.
"Could I have an ID card too?"

"All right," said Sergeant Paterson. "But I don't want all your friends coming in here, asking for IDs. This is just between us. A strictly professional matter. Is that clear?"

"Yes, sir," said Martin.

"We'll only show the ID cards to our two assistants," Pauline assured him.

"Keep up the good work!" said the sergeant.

The telephone rang. Suddenly Sergeant Paterson had urgent business to attend to. "I'm on my way!" he said, putting the phone down. He shouted to the other policemen: "We're needed at the train station. There's been another raid!" He grabbed his jacket and ran out, muttering, "That's the second this month!"

Three short rings, then two long. That was their secret signal to Philip and Julia.

Philip and Julia ran downstairs. Julia had her binoculars with her, and Philip his magnifying glass. They went into the backyard to discuss their plan of action.

Pauline showed off her ID card.

Julia was impressed. "Wow! That looks really professional!" she said. "Can I have one too?"

"Sorry," said Martin. "We can't get any more. Will you help us anyway?"

"Of course," they both assured him. "What do you want us to do?"

"We need a photograph of the wallet," said Martin.

"I can take one with my Polaroid camera," Julia said.

"And a photo of the coat," said Pauline. "So we can show it to people, and see if anyone knows who it belongs to."

"And in your spare time you can keep watch outside Mega Mart," said Martin.

"If an old lady with some sort of a cane and a black-and-white dog turns up," he went on, "ask her if she's lost her wallet."

The assistants nodded.

"The oak tree in the car park would make a good observation post," Martin told them.

Sergeant Paterson's worst fears were confirmed.

The photograph of the wallet had been on display at the supermarket for only two days, but more than fifty people had come to claim it.

Only two of them had lost dry cleaning tickets as well, and they weren't from the Blue Angel.

6 Hot on the Trail!

Martin and his friends went to see Mrs.
Marks again. They showed her their ID
cards and asked to have another look
at the coat.

Mrs. Marks was impressed with the ID
cards. She got the coat at once.

"It's awfully small," said Pauline. "So
she can't be very tall."

Mrs. Marks let Philip stand on the
counter, wearing the coat, while Julia took
a photo. Martin examined the coat with
Philip's magnifying glass, which magnified
better than his own.

"She has grey hair," he noted when he
found one in a seam.

"That's right! I remember now," said
Mrs. Marks. "She had grey hair and
glasses, and wore a hearing aid."

"We're making progress!" said Martin.

Martin and Pauline went to visit the
optician, while Julia and Philip took up
their post in the oak tree outside the
supermarket.

The optician said he certainly did remember an old lady with a stick and a hearing aid who had a black-and-white dog. "Her name is Hilda Brewer," he said. He looked through his card index. "She lives at 19 Canal Walk."

"That would be her!" said Pauline excitedly. "Canal Walk is where we—I mean Martin—found her wallet!"

"Her wallet? Mrs. Brewer will be glad!" said the optician.

Martin and Pauline ran all the way to Canal Walk.

They rang the bell marked BREWER on the first floor of number 19.

But no one came to the door.

The two detectives looked at each other and sighed.

"Professional detectives don't give up as easily as this," said Martin, and he rang the bell next door.

A dog barked.

Finally a woman opened the door.

"Mrs. Brewer? She was taken to the hospital!" she informed them. "She fell outside the front door and broke her leg. I'm looking after her dog while she's away."

Pauline stroked the friendly black-and-white dog.

"Can you tell us if Mrs. Brewer has a brown coat that looks like this?" asked Martin, showing her the photo.

"Yes, that certainly is Mrs. Brewer's coat," said the woman. "But she wasn't wearing it when she had the accident."

"Of course not. It was at the cleaner's," said Martin.

"How do you know all this?" asked the woman, amazed.

"We found Mrs. Brewer's wallet, and the dry-cleaning ticket was in it."

"She will be pleased. When her wallet disappeared after the accident, she thought someone had stolen it." Then she said, "Why don't you call her? I have the telephone number for the hospital."

"We certainly will!" said Martin, and he wrote down the number.

7   Raid at the Supermarket

"We'd better tell Julia and Philip the case is solved," said Pauline. "We can't leave them sitting in that tree all day like a pair of squirrels."

"Hey!" said Martin as they reached Tower Street. "Look at that van over there! It's the one we saw outside your grandmother's house!"

"So what?" said Pauline. "The driver stopped at a red light. Everyone does. There's nothing suspicious about that. Come on, let's find Julia and Philip."

Outside Mega Mart, Julia ran towards them, puffing and panting.

"I was just buying ice cream for me and Philip," she gasped. "And a man with a Mickey Mouse mask pushed past me and grabbed a silver suitcase from that man over there! I saw it all!"

Julia pointed at a group of people on the other side of the road. They had gathered around the security guard from the supermarket. A siren wailed. A police car roared up and Sergeant Paterson jumped out.

Martin ran over to him.

"My friend Julia saw what happened, Sergeant!"

"Hang on! I have to speak to the security guard first," said the sergeant.

Then Philip ran up. "The robber ran to Tower Street!" he shouted. "He threw away the mask and jumped into a blue van!"

Philip pointed at the oak tree. "I was up there with my binoculars. I saw it all!"

"A blue van? Tower Street? I think I can give you the plate number, Sergeant!"

Martin rummaged in his pocket for the movie ticket.

"Brilliant!" said Sergeant Paterson. "Now we'll catch him. This is the third attack on a security guard this month!"

8 The Black Glove

The van was traced within half an hour, but the driver insisted that the raid on the supermarket had nothing to do with him. He denied he'd ever left anything in a shed, either, though the children had already told the police where to find the loot from the other raids.

"Yes, that's the man! We saw him run into the shed with a silver briefcase!" said Pauline confidently. "He was wearing exactly the same jacket."

"The kid's lying," spluttered the man. "Hundreds of people have jackets like this."

"I can prove it was him!" said Martin, who could see something black sticking out of the man's jacket pocket. Martin pulled it out with a flourish. It was a black glove!

"That's mine! Give it back!" snarled the man. He lunged at Martin, scowling furiously.

"Just as I thought, it's a right glove," Martin announced. "I found the matching left glove outside the shed where he hid the loot!" He pulled the proof from his pocket. "This is the man with the black glove!"

"Good work, young detectives!" said Sergeant Paterson, giving Martin an appreciative pat on the shoulder. "I think we can say we have solved this case."

"Not only this one!" said Martin, smiling proudly. "We've solved two cases! We found the owner of the wallet, too! Oops, that reminds me. We have to call Mrs. Brewer."

About the Author

Ursel Scheffler was born in Nuremberg, a German city where many toys are made. She has written over one hundred children's books, which have been published in fifteen different languages. Her other easy-to-read books for North-South are the first book featuring Martin Pitman, *The Spy in the Attic*; *Grandpa's Amazing Computer*; and a trio of adventures featuring a sly fox and a duck detective: *Rinaldo, the Sly Fox*; *The Return of Rinaldo, the Sly Fox*; and *Rinaldo on the Run*.

About the Illustrator

Christa Unzner was born in a town near Berlin, Germany. She had always wanted to be a ballet dancer, but she ended up studying commercial art and working in an advertising agency.

Winning third prize in a book illustration contest led her to a career as a freelance illustrator, primarily of children's books. Her previous easy-to-read books for North-South are *The Spy in the Attic* by Ursel Scheffler, *Loretta and the Little Fairy* by Gerda Marie Scheidl, and *Jasmine & Rex* by Wolfram Hänel.

NORTH-SOUTH PAPERBACK EASY-TO-READ BOOKS

Abby
by Wolfram Hänel
illustrated by Alan Marks

Bear at the Beach
by Clay Carmichael

The Ghost in the Classroom
by Gerda Wagener
illustrated by Uli Waas

Harry's Got a Girlfriend!
by Ulli Schubert
illustrated by Wolfgang Slawski

Leave It to the Molesons!
by Burny Bos
illustrated by Hans de Beer

Lila's Little Dinosaur
by Wolfram Hänel
illustrated by Alex de Wolf

**Little Polar Bear and
the Brave Little Hare**
by Hans de Beer

Loretta and the Little Fairy
by Gerda Marie Scheidl
illustrated by Christa Unzner-Fischer

Mary and the Mystery Dog
by Wolfram Hänel
illustrated by Kirsten Höcker

Meet the Molesons
by Burny Bos
illustrated by Hans de Beer

Mia the Beach Cat
by Wolfram Hänel
illustrated by Kirsten Höcker

Midnight Rider
by Krista Ruepp
illustrated by Ulrike Heyne

More from the Molesons
by Burny Bos
illustrated by Hans de Beer

A Mouse in the House!
by Gerda Wagener
illustrated by Uli Waas

The Old Man and the Bear
by Wolfram Hänel
illustrated by Jean-Pierre Corderoc'h

Rescue at Sea!
by Wolfram Hänel
illustrated by Ulrike Heyne

The Return of Rinaldo, the Sly Fox
by Ursel Scheffler
illustrated by Iskender Gider

Rinaldo on the Run
by Ursel Scheffler
illustrated by Iskender Gider

Rinaldo, the Sly Fox
by Ursel Scheffler
illustrated by Iskender Gider

Spiny
by Jürgen Lassig
illustrated by Uli Waas

The Spy in the Attic
by Ursel Scheffler
illustrated by Christa Unzner

The Upside-Down Reader
by Wilhelm Gruber
illustrated by Marlies Rieper-Bastian

Used-Up Bear
by Clay Carmichael

Where's Molly?
by Uli Waas